For Cheri — W. B.   To Ammon and Chloe — K. H.

Text copyright © 2018 by Wade Bradford. Illustrations copyright © 2018 by Kevin Hawkes. All rights reserved. No part of this book may be reproduced, transmitted, or stored in an information retrieval system in any form or by any means, graphic, electronic, or mechanical, including photocopying, taping, and recording, without prior written permission from the publisher. First edition 2018. Library of Congress Catalog Card Number pending. ISBN 978-0-7636-8665-9. This book was typeset in ITC Espirit. The illustrations were done in acrylic and ink. Candlewick Press, 99 Dover Street, Somerville, Massachusetts 02144. visit us at www.candlewick.com. Printed in Dongguan, Guangdong, China. 18 19 20 21 22 23 TLF 10 9 8 7 6 5 4 3 2 1

THERE'S A DINOSAUR ON THE 13TH FLOOR

Wade Bradford ~ illustrated by Kevin Hawkes

CANDLEWICK PRESS

"Welcome to the Sharemore Hotel," said the bellhop.
"You must be Mr. Snore. Let me show you to your room."

"The sooner the better," said Mr. Snore.
"I am very"—YAWN—"sleepy."

"Here you are," said the bellhop. "Room 104.
  Sweet dreams, Mr. Snore."

Mr. Snore thanked the bellhop, got ready for bed,
crawled under the covers, and switched off the light.

But as he was about to lay his head upon the pillow,
he heard a squeaking sound.

"Hello, front desk? This is Mr. Snore in room 104. Somebody is sleeping on my pillow."

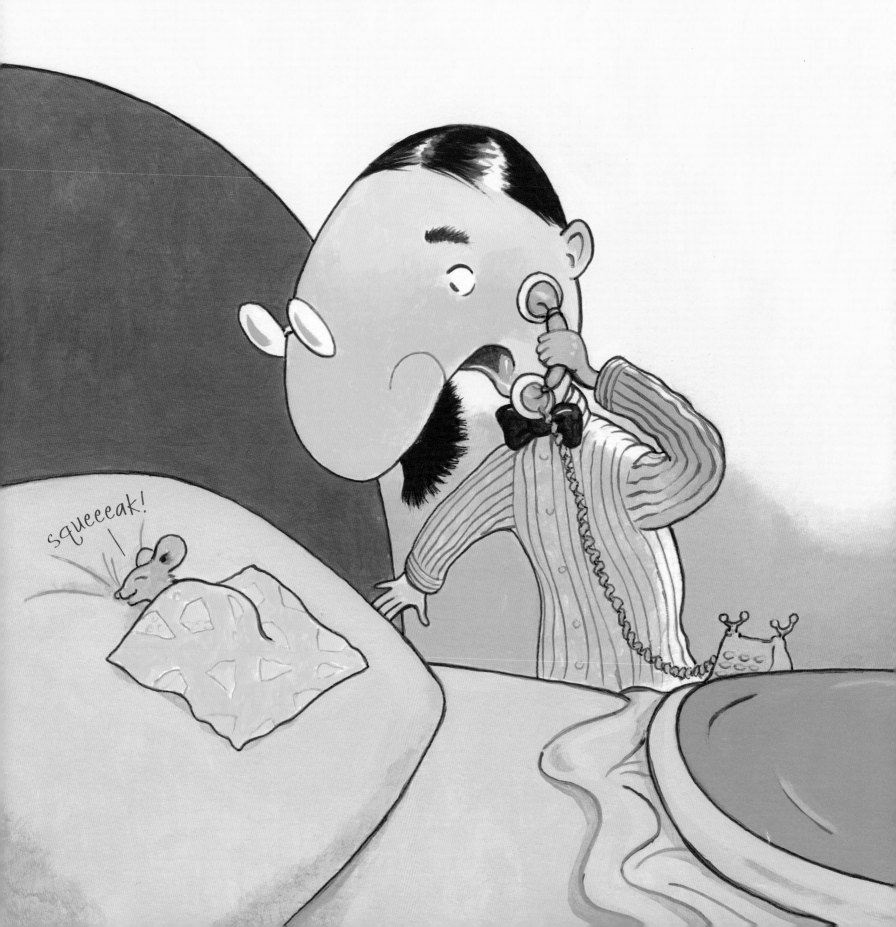

"Yes, that would be the mouse," said the bellhop.
"I believe he has had a very long day."

"So have I," grumbled Mr. Snore. "And I do not wish
to share a room with a mouse!"

So the bellhop led Mr. Snore to a room on the second floor. "Sleep tight, Mr. Snore."

Mr. Snore crawled into bed and switched off the light,
but just as he was falling asleep, he felt a rush of cold air.

Mr. Snore called the front desk again. "Someone is hogging all the covers!"

"That would be the pig," said the bellhop. "Shall I bring you
    another blanket?"

"No!" Mr. Snore fumed. "I want another room!"

So the bellhop took Mr. Snore to the third floor . . . where there were no pigs or mice to be found.

Mr. Snore kicked off his slippers, crawled into bed, and was just about to close his eyes when . . .

"Sorry about the leaky ceiling," the bellhop said as Mr. Snore marched past the ocean view on the fourth floor.

"This time," declared Mr. Snore, "I will find my own room."

He found one on the fifth floor.

"I don't think you will like this room," whispered the bellhop.
"Unless, of course, you are fond of —"

"Spiders!" cried Mr. Snore.

"Quick," said the bellhop. "To the elevator!"

"How do you feel about bees?" asked the bellhop.

"The same way I feel about spiders," said Mr. Snore.
"Please skip the sixth floor."

The seventh floor was too hot. The eighth floor was too cold.
The ninth floor was just —

"Giraffes!" cried Mr. Snore.

The bellhop smiled.
"Would you care to guess what's
on the tenth floor?"

On the tenth floor, they found . . .

"Hamsters! Where are
the rest of the giraffes?"
asked Mr. Snore.

"On the eleventh floor," said the bellhop.

"Then I will stay on the twelfth," said Mr. Snore.

So they went to the twelfth floor. "Hey, it's empty,"
said Mr. Snore.

"No one ever stays here," explained the bellhop.

"Perfect," said Mr. Snore, and he lay down and shut his eyes.

"It does tend to get a bit noisy," the bellhop warned,
but Mr. Snore was already fast asleep.

STOMP,
STOMP,
STOMP!
Gurgle,
Gurgle.
SWISH,
SWISH.

Mr. Snore rang the front desk.

"I cannot sleep with all this noise! I'm going to find a room on the thirteenth floor."

"Oh, dear, no!" said the bellhop. "On the thirteenth floor there is a—"

Click!

Mr. Snore did not wait to hear the bellhop's warning.
He went up to the thirteenth floor.

There were no mice, no pigs, no penguins, no snakes,
no spiders, no dolphins, no bees, and no giraffes.
Not even a hint of a hamster.

Nothing but a giant room with a giant bed and a giant pillow.

"I do hope Mr. Snore will be all right," said the bellhop.

Ring! went the phone at the front desk of the Sharemore Hotel.

"Hello. This is the dinosaur on the thirteenth floor.
Somebody is sleeping on my pillow!"

The bellhop sighed. "That would be Mr. Snore,"
he said. "He has had a very long day."

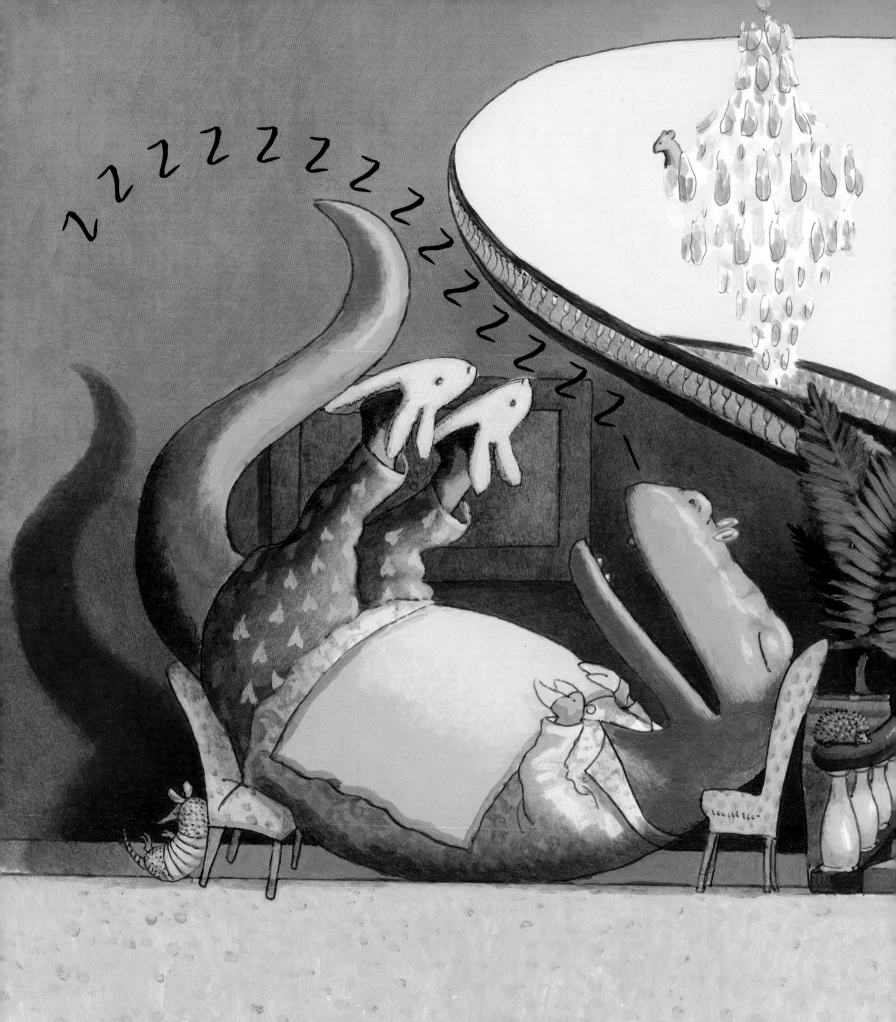